STARSHIP
RESCUE

by T. Breslin

illustrated by Harriet Buckley

Librarian Reviewer

Marci Peschke

Librarian, Dallas Independent School District

MA Education Reading Specialist, Stephen F. Austin State University

Learning Resources Endorsement, Texas Women's University

Reading Consultant

Elizabeth Stedem

Educator/Consultant, Colorado Springs, CO

MA in Elementary Education, University of Denver, CO

STONE ARCH BOOKS

MINNEAPOLIS   SAN DIEGO

First published in the United States in 2007
by Stone Arch Books,
151 Good Counsel Drive, P.O. Box 669,
Mankato, Minnesota 56002.
www.stonearchbooks.com

Published by arrangement with
Barrington Stoke Ltd, Edinburgh.

Library of Congress Cataloging-in-Publication Data
Breslin, Theresa.
    Starship Rescue / by T. Breslin; illustrated by Harriet Buckley.
    p. cm. — (Pathway Books)
    Summary: Marc lives with a band of Outsiders on a distant planet but
when he tries to find a way to outwit the planet's evil leader, he encounters a
problem with someone he thought he could trust.
    ISBN-13: 978-1-59889-107-2 (hardcover)
    ISBN-10: 1-59889-107-3 (hardcover)
    ISBN-13: 978-1-59889-267-3 (paperback)
    ISBN-10: 1-59889-267-3 (paperback)
    [1. Science fiction.] I. Buckley, Harriet, 1974–, ill. II. Title. III. Series.
PZ7.B7545St 2007
[Fic]—dc22   2006005069

Art Director: Heather Kindseth
Cover Graphic Designer and Illustrator: Brann Garvey
Interior Graphic Designer: Kay Fraser

1 2 3 4 5 6 11 10 09 08 07 06

Printed in the United States of America.

TABLE OF CONTENTS

CHAPTER 1

OUTSIDE THE FORTRESS

Ten seconds. Just ten seconds.

That was all the time Marc was going to have. Con, their leader, made that very clear. The spy, Alex, had sent them a message. Tonight, the Keepers of the Fortress would change the patrol on the main gate just before the planet's two suns set. It would be safe to cross the wall beside the gate then. But only for ten seconds.

"Ten seconds," Con said again. "That is how long the killer electric beam will be switched off to let the guards out and in. A red light will come on. The guards will be given ten seconds to change over, and then the electric beam will be turned back on again."

He gazed deep into Marc's eyes.

"They tell me that you can run fast, Marc. Let's hope that's true."

Marc listened with great care as Con told him what he had to do. Marc was wearing an anti-gravity belt. The belt would lift him up and over the wall in a few seconds. Then Marc would take the message capsule to Con, who would be waiting for him in the main square.

"You've looked at the map?" Con asked him. "Do you know the way?"

Marc nodded. He knew exactly what he had to do. He also knew danger was part of the plan. Con turned to the rest of the Outsiders huddling in the caves beside the Merkonium mines.

"Our time has come," Con said. "For too long Jared and the Keepers have kept us on the outside as slaves in the mines. Tomorrow night, the *Starship* from our planet, Earth, will fly close to our world, as it does every 20 years. The message capsule, which Marc will bring into the Fortress, will send an SOS to them."

"If only they took the time to beam down on us as they passed," said one of the Outsiders.

"Then they would see how we have to slave away in the Merkonium mines, while the Keepers and the Chosen Ones have an easy life inside the Fortress," said another Outsider.

"Yes," said another. "It's time they knew how Jared, the evil Keeper, has destroyed this planet, which was once so beautiful."

Con held up his hand for silence. "It will all end soon," said Con. "Tomorrow morning, I will get into the Fortress with my pass. As you all know, they let a few of us go in and out of the Fortress to buy and sell. But we have to be screened in the X-ray booth before we can enter. The message capsule would be found if I took it in with me."

The Outsiders nodded as Con spoke.

"We have to make sure that the capsule gets to the Radio Control Station in the Fortress," said Con. "Marc will carry it across the wall to me. Then we will go to the radio control station, place it in the transmitter, and send out our call for help"

* * *

The Outsiders' meeting had taken place during the morning. That afternoon, Marc hid in the bushes outside the Fortress. He looked at his watch. Five more minutes to wait. He was not close to the wall. Could he reach it in time?

He knew why he had been chosen. He was small, so he could hide easily. He also didn't weigh much, so the anti-gravity belt would quickly lift him over the wall.

He had been hiding in the bushes all day. It was almost time. The planet's two suns were low in the sky. In one minute, the Keepers would turn off the electric beam. The red light would come on. Then there would be just ten seconds for the old patrol guards to go into the Fortress and the new guards to come out.

Marc counted the seconds on his watch.

14 . . . 13 . . . 12 . . .

Marc got ready to go.

11 . . .

His heart jumped. The red warning light went on at the gate.

It was time to run.

10!

CHAPTER 2

FREEDOM RUN

Marc ran toward the wall. As he ran, he counted. "9 . . . 8 . . . 7 . . ."

Marc got to the high wall of the Fortress. He pressed the button on his anti-gravity belt and flew upward.

"4 . . . 3 . . ." He counted. The wall went on and on. "2 . . ."

He was at the top. Marc pressed a second button and shot forward.

He was over the top of the wall. No time for a careful landing. He crashed to the ground.

He stood up as fast as he could and limped toward some thick bushes. As he crawled into them, Marc felt for the message capsule inside his pocket. It was safe!

He heard someone call, "This way!"

The sound of running feet crashed through the night. Two Keepers were standing at the spot where Marc had come over the wall.

"I'm sure I heard something," said one of the Keepers.

"Maybe over there," said the other. He pointed at Marc's hiding place. "In those bushes?"

CHAPTER 3

SASHA

Marc was scared. The Keepers were walking toward his hiding place!

Marc felt a sharp tug on the hood of his cloak.

"I'm Sasha. Follow me," a voice said in his ear.

He looked around and saw a short girl with dark hair standing just behind him. She wore the purple cloak of the Chosen Ones.

"Hurry!" she whispered.

She ran swiftly through the trees, and Marc followed her.

They soon came to the first houses in the city. Each house was surrounded by a high wooden fence. Sasha went up to one of the fences and put her hand on it. Part of the fence slid to one side. "In you go," she said.

Sasha slipped through after him and closed the fence up again. "That should slow them down," she said.

Marc hadn't been inside the Fortress before. He had never seen anything so wonderful. The gardens were full of flowers. The walls of the houses and offices looked pink in the light from the setting suns.

They walked for a little ways before the girl turned to Marc.

"Do you have the SOS message capsule?" she asked

Marc's hands were damp with fear. "I don't know what you are talking about," he said.

"We don't have time to play games," Sasha said. "Do you have the SOS message from the Outsiders?"

Marc said nothing.

Sasha smiled. "I know you're wondering if you can trust me."

"How do I know?" Marc asked.

She grinned at him. "You can't. Not for sure." She looked at Marc for a long moment.

"I will show that *I* trust *you*. I will tell you who I am," said Sasha.

"You've told me who you are. You said your name is Sasha," said Marc.

"Yes, I am Sasha," said the girl, "but I am Alex, too."

"Alex?" cried Marc. "Alex, the spy? The one inside the Fortress who tells the Outsiders what is going on?"

"Yes," said Sasha. "Everyone inside the Fortress calls me Sasha. But I use the name Alex when I send news to the Outsiders."

Marc waited, still not sure. "I only know you as Sasha," he said. "I still don't know if I can trust you."

"Look," said Sasha. "There's nothing else you can do. You have to trust me."

CHAPTER 4

INSIDE THE FORTRESS

After a pause, Marc said, "Okay.
I guess you're right. Yes, I have the
message capsule."

"Then we must hurry," said Sasha.
"The streets won't be safe for long.
Everyone must be back in their own
homes just one hour after the suns set.
Anyone still in the streets after that will
be arrested."

She walked down the street.

Marc waited a moment before
heading after her. He pulled Sasha into a
doorway where they would not be seen.

"This isn't the way to the main square," said Marc.

"We're not going there," said Sasha.

"Con said I must go to the main square," said Marc.

"No," said Sasha. "We are going to the radio control station. We can put the message capsule in the transmitter there and send it out to the *Starship*."

"How can we get into the radio control station?" asked Marc.

"I can get us both inside," said Sasha, "as long as we get there before dark."

Marc shook his head. He didn't want to follow Sasha. He had to meet Con in the main square. He must go there first.

"How do I get to the main square?" he asked Sasha.

"That way," Sasha told him.

Marc was about to step out from the doorway when Sasha pulled him back. Some Keepers walked by the entry.

"There are more of them around tonight," said Sasha. Marc could see she was scared. "We must hurry to the radio control station."

"No," said Marc. "I'm not going anywhere until I've seen Con."

Sasha turned and looked at him.

"Don't you know?" she said. "Con was arrested."

CHAPTER 5

CON

"No!" cried Marc. He felt as if he had been hit.

"I'm sorry," said Sasha. "I thought you knew."

"I've been hiding in the bushes all day," said Marc. "There's no way that I could have known that Con was arrested."

"Everyone in the Fortress is talking about it," said Sasha.

"That is why I came to find you at the wall. Jared will force Con to tell him the truth," she added.

Sasha took Marc's arm. "You see now why we must hurry. Soon, Con will tell Jared everything."

"He'll never talk," said Marc.

Sasha looked at Marc. "Those who are taken by Jared the Keeper," she said, "all talk in the end."

"We have to rescue him," Marc said.

Sasha shook her head. "It is no good. Even I cannot get past the prison guards."

"We've got to try," said Marc.

What will the Outsiders do without Con? Marc wondered.

Marc felt sick. Con was their leader. This plan was his. He'd made them think that they could get a message to the *Starship* as it passed. If he had been arrested, then there was no hope.

"I'm going to free him," said Marc.

"Just how will you do that?" asked Sasha. "He's in the prison. Only Keepers can go in and out, and they are checked at six different gates."

"I don't care," said Marc. "He has done so much for us. I must help him."

"You don't understand, do you?" Sasha said.

"No!" yelled Marc. "It is you who doesn't understand! You are one of the Chosen Ones. You have a fine life. We work in the mines all day. You are never hungry or cold. Look at your warm clothes, and then look at what I wear."

He showed her the dirty, torn clothes he was wearing.

"There's no time to argue," Sasha told him.

"We must go to the radio control station now," she said.

"You're right," said Marc. "I won't argue with you. But I'm going to the prison now."

Sasha blocked his way.

"Listen to me," she said. "You have the message capsule. It must be sent out tonight. If you go to the prison, you may be arrested, too. Think about it. What would Con want you to do?"

CHAPTER 6

A DISAGREEMENT

"He would want me to help him escape," Marc said at once. "He would want to be free."

"I would like to be free, too," said Sasha sadly.

Marc laughed. "You are free. You live in the Fortress."

"Yes," said Sasha. "I live in the Fortress. But I am not free."

"We are all scared here," explained the girl. "There are spies all around us. We cannot say what we want, or go where we please. We trust no one. They choose the movies we see and the books we read."

"What!" said Marc. "You would rather live on the Outside where nothing grows, no grass, no trees?"

"Perhaps," said Sasha. "It was beautiful a long time ago, before the Keepers destroyed it all. It could be that way again if the Outsiders and the people in the Fortress work together."

"But first we must get rid of the Keepers," said Marc.

"Yes, we must," said Sasha.

CHAPTER 7

JARED THE KEEPER

Marc nodded. "You're right," he said.

Sasha took his arm. "This way," she said.

Marc kept his hood up as he and Sasha walked through the side streets.

No one stopped them. Everyone was hurrying to get back home before dark.

Marc and Sasha arrived at the radio control station.

"Here we are," said Sasha. "The gate will open when you put this card in the slot."

She gave Marc a thin plastic card.

"Where did you get this?" asked Marc.

Sasha smiled. "There are others in the Fortress who want to help us. Now, when we get inside, we'll go to the basement. We can creep along the air ducts until we reach the room where they send out the electronic messages."

Ten minutes later, Sasha and Marc were crawling along the air ducts. The passages were filthy and full of twists and turns. Sasha went first, as quick as a cat. After several minutes, she stopped beside a metal grid.

She looked carefully through the bars of the grid.

"Here," she said softly. "My spies say that just after the suns set, the man in charge has a ten minute break. We'll wait."

This is worse than hiding in the bushes all day, thought Marc. They didn't dare move. They listened and waited.

Sasha put her hand on his arm. "He left the room," she said. She took a sharp tool from under her cloak and, with Marc's help, opened the metal grid. They climbed down into the room.

"The transmitter is right there," said Sasha, pointing to a platform.

"Let's send the message now," said Marc.

He got out the capsule from his shirt. Sasha took it from him.

"So small, yet so important," Marc said softly.

Marc heard a noise outside the door. He grabbed Sasha's arm. "Listen," he said. They heard footsteps. "Someone's coming," said Marc.

Sasha peeked through the glass panel at the top of the door. She turned to Marc. She was shaking. "Oh no!" she cried. "It's Jared the Keeper!" She shrank behind the door as it was flung open. A tall man stood in the doorway.

"Hello, Marc," he said. "We meet again."

"Con!" Marc shouted out. "You're free! How did you escape?"

Then Marc saw that Con was not smiling. His face was grim.

"It was very easy to escape," said Con. "I have my own key. The prison belongs to me."

"What do you mean?" asked Marc.

Suddenly, Marc understood what Sasha had said before she hid behind the door. "Oh no! It is Jared!"

"Let me tell you who I am, boy," said the man. "I am Con to you. But I am also Jared the Keeper."

CHAPTER 8

BETRAYED

Marc fell back.

"Is this a trick?" he gasped.

"Yes, it is," said Jared. "And it's a very
good one. Let me explain it to you, boy."
He came closer to Marc. "The Outsiders
know that a ship from Earth comes close
to our planet every twenty years." Jared
spoke very slowly. "We, the Keepers,
know the Outsiders know this."

"Every twenty years we expect the Outsiders to try to send an SOS to the ship from Earth," said Jared.

He sneered at Marc. "This time, I didn't wait for the Outsiders to try to get a message out. I decided to plan it myself. This way, I would know exactly what you were all up to."

"You betrayed us!" cried Marc.

"You could say that," said Jared. "But I think that I have saved you, too. In the past, lots of Outsiders died when they attacked the Fortress. My plan has stopped all that."

"Why did you let me get this far?" Marc said. He began to sob.

"I didn't think you'd ever make it to the radio control station," said Jared.

"You should have been arrested at the gate, or in the main square," said the man. "When no one saw you there, I came here to check, just in case you got inside the transmitting room."

"Why didn't you stick to the plan to meet me in the main square?" asked Marc. "Why did you make everyone think that Con was in prison?"

"I didn't want people to see me with you in the square. Many in the Fortress know what Jared looks like. No one must find out that Con and Jared are the same person. I want to be able to go back to the Outsiders as Con. I will tell them that the plan failed."

Jared paused, and gave Marc a wicked smile.

"And then I will help them make a new plan for the next time a ship comes," he said.

"You won't always win," Marc told him. "Next time someone smarter will take my place."

"Don't be too hard on yourself, boy," said Jared. "You did very well to get this far. I thought that you would go to the main square, or, if you heard Con was in prison, you would go there to rescue him."

"I planned to go," said Marc, "but I decided to follow the plan."

He stopped talking. Sasha! It was Sasha who stopped him from trying to rescue Con. It was Sasha who helped him get here. Where was she? What was she doing?

Jared went on. "I will deal with you, and then I must find out who this spy is. But first, give me the message."

"It's probably a fake," said Marc.

"No," said Jared. "You Outsiders know about electronics. You would know if the message was a fake. The message capsule itself is real."

Marc held his breath. Sasha had the message capsule! Jared had not seen her. He did not know who the spy called Alex was. He did not know about Sasha! There was still hope!

"Give me the capsule," said Jared.

"What?" said Marc, trying to delay Jared. Sasha was creeping along the wall to the transmitter.

She had the message capsule in her hand. She was going to try to send the message! Marc saw that he needed to stall a little longer.

Marc looked back at Jared. "But I still don't understand," he said.

"There is nothing more for you to understand, boy," said Jared angrily. "Give me the message capsule."

"No," said Marc.

"This is stupid," said Jared. "You have nothing to gain by keeping it." He pulled his laser gun from his belt. "Give it to me."

"I'd rather die," said Marc.

"Then die you will," said Jared, and he lifted his arm to shoot.

CHAPTER 9

STARSHIP RESCUE

"You'll die with me," said Marc.

"What do you mean?" asked Jared.

"You can't fire a laser gun in here," said Marc. "This room's too small."

Jared shook his head. "You're wrong," he said.

Marc was frantic. He had to keep Jared talking. He spoke fast. "In such a small space the blast would be huge. It would kill us both."

"No, you're wrong," said Jared. "And you know it." He stared at Marc for a moment, looking puzzled. "You're only stalling. Why?"

Marc stared back.

"Why?" Jared asked again. "Why are you trying to delay me?"

Marc said nothing.

Jared stepped across the room and grabbed Marc's arm. "Give me the message capsule. Now!"

Marc tried to escape, but Jared's grip was firm.

As he tried to get free, Marc saw Sasha race to the transmitter platform.

But as Marc saw her, so did Jared.

"Ah!" he yelled. "Now I see what this is all about! There's another traitor in here!"

He raised his laser gun and took aim at the girl.

"Stand back from the transmitter!" he yelled at Sasha. "Stand back or I'll fire!"

Sasha turned. She had opened the sending slot at the front of the transmitter.

All she had to do now was drop the message capsule inside, close the slot, and press the start button. It would only take about three seconds. But Sasha realized that it was three seconds she did not have.

Her hand, holding the capsule, fell to her side.

Jared smiled. "Well done," he said.

Marc's body went limp. It was all over. The Outsiders had lost again. Jared released his grip on Marc's arm.

Then Marc saw Sasha's arm move. She had been bluffing so Jared wouldn't shoot at her.

She was going to do it!

"Stupid girl," Jared shouted at her.

Jared fired his laser gun, but as he did, Marc jumped up and knocked it out of his hand.

Sasha yelled as she was hit. She clutched her arm. The capsule fell from her hand and rolled across the floor.

Jared bent down to pick up his laser gun. Marc kicked it away. Jared went after it, and Marc ran to help Sasha. She picked up the capsule. "Don't think about me," she said, sobbing. "Send the message."

Marc grabbed the capsule from her and put it in the sending slot.

"Press that button and I will kill you." Jared came toward him.

Marc looked at him. "Too late," he said as he pressed the button.

Silence filled the room. Jared's face was hard and angry.

"You're too late, Jared," Marc said again. "Even if you fired your gun, the message would still be sent. We both know that it only takes a microsecond to transmit."

Jared gave a twisted smile. "So, in the end, you were the smart one, boy." He backed away from Sasha and Marc.

"Now, I think I'll go," he said.

"Stay where you are!" said someone behind him.

Four officers wearing Starfleet Security uniforms came into the room.

"I'm Captain Mary Rand, Head of Security on *Starship*," said one of the officers. "We came down to answer a call for help. Who can tell me what's going on here?"

Marc looked around. Two of the team took Jared's gun from him. The other officer was checking the laser burn on Sasha's arm.

"I can try," said Marc.

 # MISSION OVER?

"This is the life for me," Marc told Sasha later.

Sasha rested in the hospital while her burn healed. Marc stood beside her bed eating an orange.

On a table in front of him was a bowl with different kinds of fruit. Every so often Marc picked one up, studying it carefully. "I've never seen so much fruit," he said.

Sasha smiled.

"Please stop talking about food for one minute and tell me what's going on in the Fortress," she said.

"Starfleet Security has taken over," said Marc. "They are setting up a new ruling council. The Outsiders and the people in the Fortress will work together. The Keepers have all been arrested."

"Where's Jared now?" asked Sasha.

"He's been taken to the *Starship*," said Marc. "They say that he'll be sent back to Earth to be tried and punished."

"Our work is done," Sasha said.

Marc bit into an apple. He grinned at Sasha. "I think it may have just begun," he said.

★ About The Author

Theresa Breslin became a writer by accident. She was a traveling librarian, and was very annoyed about an injustice taking place in one of the towns she visited. She wrote a book about it with a young boy as the main character. It won an award and was filmed for television. And suddenly she was a writer!

★ About The Illustrator

Harriet Buckley is a very busy artist. After earning a master's degree in illustration at the Edinburgh College of Art in Scotland, she has worked non-stop illustrating books, magazines, and comics. Harriet likes creating artwork digitally on computers, and has also animated numerous commercials and short films. She has even painted an "optical illusion"-style mural for a private home in Holland.

★ Glossary

bluffing (BLUHF-ing)—pretending to be stronger than you really are or to know more than you really do

ducts (DUHKTS)—tubes or vents that carry air from one place to another inside a building

filthy (FILTH-ee)—dirty

grid (GRID)—a set of straight lines that cross each other to form a pattern of squares

grim (GRIM)—gloomy, stern

huddling (HUHD-ling)—crowding together in a tight group

slumped (SLUMPT)—sank down heavily and suddenly

SOS (ESS-OH-ESS)—a call for help. Some people think the letters come from the message "**S**ave **O**ur **S**hip."

transmit (tranz-MIT)—to send a message, usually electronically or through radio signals

★ Discussion Questions

1. In what ways is the term Outsiders an appropriate name for the members of Marc's group? In what ways is it inappropriate?

2. Why do you think Marc decides to put his faith in Sasha? How do you decide if a person is someone that you can trust?

 Writing Prompts

1. Marc would not have been successful in his mission if Sasha hadn't appeared to help him. Describe a time when you were successful because you partnered with someone.

2. Describe how you think life will change for the Outsiders now that the Security Council is creating a new set of rules.

★ Internet Sites

Do you want to know more about subjects related to this book? Or are you interested in learning about other topics? Then check out FactHound, a fun, easy way to find Internet sites.

Our investigative staff has already sniffed out great sites for you!

Here's how to use FactHound:

1. Visit *www.facthound.com*

2. Select your grade level.

3. To learn more about subjects related to this book, type in the book's ISBN number: **1598891073**.

4. Click the **Fetch It** button.

FactHound will fetch the best Internet sites for you!